Flickertail

by Carolyn Sherwin Bailey

pictures by Garry MacKenzie

New York   ·   Henry Z. Walck, Inc.   ·   1962

To James Hitchcock
with gratitude

Contents

1 · *The Stranger*

THEY SAT, a picnicking family of gray squirrels, on the door-stone of the Old Place in the village, eating small green apples. That is, they were chewing up the apple part, spitting it out, and eating only the small black seeds that they looked on as a treat. Footsteps of many children and grownups going in and out of the Old Place had worn a hollow in the door-stone that now held fresh water from a recent shower. From this they drank now and then. It was early summer and a sunny day. The sky could not have been bluer. They were old residents of the ancient and crooked Porter apple tree that stood beside the Old Place and had held the swing for the children and grandchildren. The tree now protected the house even to the roof. Its family of two-leggers was not occupying the house this summer, vacationing at the Cape for a change.

This was the Nutting family of squirrels, residents there for a long time. A thunderstorm had split the tree but it stood up strongly. They lived in the crotches, handy to the ground and not too far away for trips to the roof. They were Mr. and Mrs. Nutting, William the only son, Miss Bushy Nutting, a schoolteacher who lived with Grandpa Nutting at the end of the great lawn at the back of the house where there were a stand of mammoth oak trees and the children's sandbox. The sandbox was now deserted, and the squirrels used it as a kind of cafeteria; during school terms as a place for Miss Bushy's school. Miss Bushy was visiting her relatives for the picnic and taking part in the important matter they were discussing.

Between chewing, spitting and eating, they talked the thing over. Mr. Nutting spoke from his belief. His first name was Hickory and he was a squirrel of strong opinions. Going over the matter about which they were all thinking, from time to time he shook his head and chattered. When he was young and inexperienced Hickory Nutting had rashly eaten a nut, shell and all. This, it was said, had given him a hard outlook on life; the shell had entered his nature.

Hickory Nutting's chattering changed to muttering.

"There isn't one. If there were I would have seen it," he said. "And what is more I forbid any member of my family seeing things that do not exist and talking about them. Understand that once and for all." He looked sternly at Mrs. Nutting.

No one ever knew exactly what was in Mrs. Nutting's mind. She was a good wife, doing her share of gathering and storing nuts, but she had little mind of her own. She always agreed with Mr. Nutting. Now she looked at Miss Bushy. The entire family took pride in Bushy. She had taught the squirrel school for a long time and was close to the age of retirement, when she would be given an allowance of nuts; but she had no intention of giving up. Now she spoke from her experience.

"According to arithmetic," she fairly trembled with words, "if you eat more nuts than you save, you will run short in the winter." She always had advice to give and now went on. "If this family would spend more time getting ready for bad weather and less time gossiping, it would be better off. I for one have never seen what you seem to think you have seen, and I am an educated squirrel."

"Anything else, Bushy?" Mr. Nutting asked. He liked to have the last word in the family. He liked the importance of having a teacher as his sister, but found it tiresome listening to Bushy's advice day in and day out, day after day.

"Plenty," she replied. "I remember, Hickory, when you were young you were poor at arithmetic. You mixed up addition and subtraction. You ate more acorns than you buried. Many a winter day when you came down-tree, you found no food. About this matter we all have in mind, it is not spoken of in any course of study."

"True," Mr. Nutting picked up another apple and began

chewing it, "but it is worth our thought." He might have gone on, but they were interrupted. A sudden commotion called their attention to the attic window.

A flagpole extended out of the attic window toward the Porter apple tree. It almost touched the higher boughs of the tree. The attic of the Old Place was full of interesting things—old swords and rifles, clothes in which to dress up and give plays, cracked blue and white dishes for tea parties, a case of doctor's instruments for hospital play, golf clubs, tennis rackets—everything one wanted or needed. And books! There was hardly a book a person could not find in the attic of the Old Place, from the Bible that was supposed to have come over in the Mayflower to *St. Nicholas* and the works of Howard Pyle. It had been the home of mice until it had a new resident, much more appreciative.

Now out the partly opened attic window, running lightly along the flagpole, leaping into the tree, dropping onto the door-stone among his family came William S. (the S for Shakespeare), Willie Nutting, who now spent most of his time in the attic gnawing the leather bindings of the books.

They did not speak for a moment, Willie having been away for several days. They looked up to him, also, the only son and learned. It seemed as if he had taken in the meaning of the books with the bindings he ate. The Shakespeare of his name had been given him by his Aunt Bushy. If the truth were known, it is likely it would have been discovered that his reading was lighter, *Robinson Crusoe* and *Johnny Chuck*, but Willie basked in his family's approval. He broke the silence.

"Always the same old argument," he said. "Can't you think of something more important to talk about?"

"You're not one to be giving advice," Bushy asserted. "Why don't you leave your books and get to counting acorns? If you think your family is going to support you another winter in idleness, you have another thought coming."

Willie helped himself to an apple and presently spoke. "I don't say yes and I don't say no about this thing. I will admit this, though. I don't go downstairs often. I leave those rooms to the mice. But when I have called on Skunk in the cellar as I do now and then, I have heard noises. Of course Early Ford out in the barn may be honking to himself. Also the barn is old and may be rattling in the wind. Early Ford's parts are loose, and rattle; he has had a hard and risky life up and down mountains and along dirt roads for twenty years. I shouldn't blame him for honking to himself."

"There you are," Mr. Nutting said, "Willie hasn't seen it. There isn't one. Willie and I never saw one." But his words were interrupted by a newcomer. An old and breathless squirrel leaped into their midst. His eyes popped. His heart beat wildly. This was Grandpa Nutting, come up from the far end of the lawn.

He had come to the Old Place in time past, a forlorn old

squirrel, and the Nuttings had taken pity on him and fed him. Bushy ran to him. "You're too old, Grandpa, to rush so. You ought to come and go more slowly. What's the matter?"

Grandpa caught his breath. He looked behind him excitedly. "I saw it. I almost caught it." He spoke in chatters.

"There, there." Bushy offered him an apple. "You just think you did. It may have been dandelions blowing in the wind that you saw."

"So you say," he replied. "I was digging in the sandbox for a few of last fall's acorns and there it was, waiting for me to go so that it could help itself. I saw it with my own eyes."

Mr. Nutting tapped his head, meaning that Grandpa Nutting was not to be taken seriously. "Eat all you can," he said. "These little apples are all the Porter can bear now and they won't last long. It's going to be a long time until acorns begin dropping in any number again."

Discouraged, Grandpa ate. He was used to not being taken seriously when he spoke of the wonders he had seen during his long life—hummingbirds flying down to Brazil and coming back to the wild roses the next summer; blind moles digging their underground homes; grubs turning into gaudy tiger butterflies. He finished an apple. Then he carefully lifted his tail with his paw and wiped his mouth with it and brushed his whiskers. "His tail gets thinner and thinner every year," Bushy said in an aside. "If he does not see the things he thinks he does, perhaps he is jealous of the young. It has . . ." Around the corner of the house almost at the door-stone appeared an odd, dark little face.

Seeing the Nutting family, the face disappeared. But as the creature ran, they saw what Grandpa had chased, what Hickory Nutting would not admit existed, what Miss Bushy said was not in any course of study, what Willie said was not in the attic books.

Running, leaping, and waving its tail as it went was a stranger. It was without doubt a squirrel, but it had a beautiful flashing golden tail.

2 · Barn Planning

THIS WAS the first summer that the Old Place had been without a family. Year after year there had been boys and girls whose pigtails had changed to pony tails. Hoops had rolled in and out again; battledore and shuttlecock had changed to badminton. But there were always good times— bobsledding, skating, apple picking, tramping in and out of the kitchen with muddy feet, racing up and down stairs from kitchen to attic, and in the summer, wild-strawberry shortcake, blueberry pie, trout fishing and picnics.

Still, in spite of curtains being down and the furniture slip-covered, there was a special kind of life in the house now.

In the woodpile down-cellar Skunk had found a home, sheltered and safe. He was eating from a box of apples the family had stored away and forgotten. There was a small window insecurely hooked, out and in of which Skunk went when he felt the need to drink from Second Brook. His children had left to form their own families, and

Skunk was living an easy, well-earned life, secure from interference. His regular work was digging for grubs in the lawn, which was good for it; but now the grass was green like a thick carpet. Skunk did not mind being alone and idle for a while, but he did dread the winter when the family would be coming down-cellar for logs for the fireplace.

The little field mice who had come into the empty house were having a feast every day. There were cartons of crackers and boxes of raisins to open and eat from. There were also, as dessert, the beans in the children's beanbags, especially the fancy bags, stitched of red and yellow calico. One at a time the mice ate their filling, one at a time the beanbags became thinner until they collapsed. There they lay, flat and useless. But come fall, the grandmother would stuff them again.

The most important left-behind member of the family was Early Ford, the discarded family car. The old car had used to take the entire family, baskets full of chicken sandwiches, bottles of milk, several kinds of cold pies and apples—up, up a nearby mountain on a picnic. As they climbed, the town would seem smaller until it shrank to the size of the children's block houses. The narrow road was curved, but Early Ford took the curves with care and skill, having great care of its precious passengers. When they came to the top they would find a sightly spot in the sun, unpack, gather twigs and branches, build a fire for making coffee, eat and wish they never need go home.

Early Ford was now many years old and lived in the barn. The family had a new car, not trusting Early Ford to take them for the long trips as it had for so long. So there it was, next to the stall of the late Nellie, the grandmother's mare.

Now Early Ford was joined by a companion. Up from the back seat there appeared an odd figure. Anyone would have said it was a squirrel, except that it was different from any squirrel in that neighborhood. Its fur was not gray or red but a coppery color. It had ears short and pointed like a chipmunk's. Strangest of all, this creature had a golden tail. This tail was long and plumed. Even in the dimness of the barn it glowed like sunshine.

So these three, Skunk, Early Ford and Flickertail, lived there alone in the back parts of the Old Place having their own ways and manner of being understood. Sometimes Skunk wanted company and left the woodpile which had been his real home for a long time and came over to the big barn itself for a little friendly chat with Flick. Now that the better weather had come they visited more frequently, and had become better acquainted. Skunk was a friendly fellow, somewhat like a big cat in size, with long thick fur marked in black and white stripes. He was now getting somewhat gray, for he was a grandfather. His bushy tail was black and white. His eyes were sharp and keen. This day he had come for a visit.

Flickertail, the squirrel with the golden tail who had found his long way to this New Hampshire village, crawled out of the burrow he had made in the back seat of the car, Early Ford.

"Nice place you have here, Mr. Flickertail," Skunk said, poking around in the back-seat home. "Bright idea using paper bags for stuffing, plentiful and warm on a cold night."

Flickertail's fur bristled with pride. No one had ever praised him before. He jumped up beside Skunk. "Smart stripes you wear," he said, not to be outdone in compliments.

"Have you met the Nutting family?" Skunk asked.

"They don't recognize me as a squirrel," Flickertail said. "They either don't see me, my being something of a freak, or they don't believe they see me. It hurts my feelings. In this town it is a mistake to be different from the others."

"Right you are," Skunk replied, moving up beside Flick

and speaking secretly. "But I have news for you. Living so close to the house I pick up a few words now and then. You are discovered!"

"What do you mean—*discovered?*" Flickertail wanted to know.

"Your nutshells," Skunk replied. "I came to visit once when you were away. The man, that neighbor Joe who takes the cars to town, took Early Ford out. There is hardly a car hereabouts that can climb a mountain or stand a dirt road as it can. Joe holds it was a mistake for the family to buy a new one. I agree. Nothing like an old friend, I say.

But the Old Place children are growing up and getting notions. Well, halfway to town Early Ford stopped, went on, then stopped altogether.

" 'The garage for you, my friend,' Joe said. So we limped somehow into town and Early Ford was looked over. The garage man chuckled. 'So you've changed your diet, Joe,' he said.

" 'What do you mean, changed my diet?' Joe asked.

" 'Taken to nuts,' the garage man said, 'taken to nuts. The radiator cap was off, and the radiator is full of empty nut-shells. Look here. No wonder this old car wouldn't run.'

"Well, Flick, he had found your winter supply of nut-shells that you had hidden in the radiator. I suppose you should have emptied them outdoors a few at a time; but the weather was so bad. Joe will surely tell the family when they come home, and your nest will be noticed."

Flickertail's head drooped. "What can I do?" The weight of his trouble seemed unbearable. "I have always led such an irregular life, chased, not understood, homeless." Skunk shared his distress.

At last he had an idea. "I don't see anything, my friend, but for you to leave, much as I would hate to see you go. Why don't you try and find a mountain, Mr. Flick, pleasant and safe? A mountain has everything to recommend it, wild ones who are friendly, plenty of berries and nuts. This is mountain country."

"I like a mountain," Flickertail said. "I came from the

mountains out west. In Oregon," Flickertail began, "when men were coming out looking for gold, was our origin. That was in the time of my grandfathers. 'Go west, young man,' two-leggers had been told. 'Go east, Flickertails,' they told my grandfathers, although a squirrel could not have had a better place to live than we had—wild apples, berries, nuts, all of us alike and friendly. So we started east. At that time we wore yellow capes with black borders. It was a very long trip the Flickertails took. Over mountains, through woods, going across water on logs, hiding when we came to the small towns of log houses they built in those days, meeting enemy squirrels."

"Brave family!" Skunk said.

"On the way," Flickertail went on, "we lost our yellow capes with the black borders. Nowadays you never see a Flickertail with a yellow cape. But we kept our golden tails." He switched his tail over one paw and stroked it proudly. "I came to this small town and just stayed on. But everybody has always been against me. Now I feel as if I couldn't stand my life here any longer. I might start out and search for a nearby mountain. I know the advantages of a mountain—safety, berries and nuts for the taking."

"Snakes, beetles and grasshoppers," Skunk added with relish. "If you can catch one, there is nothing so tasty as a crisp grasshopper."

"I shall consider your idea, Skunk," Flickertail said gratefully.

3 · The Journey

A few days later Skunk again visited Flickertail in the barn.

"Hi, Mr. Flick," Skunk greeted him as he saw Flick's odd little face and pointed ears at the door of Early Ford. "I've been thinking about your finding a new home on a nearby mountain. I have been thinking of leaving, too, of starting a new life. There is little for me to do here, now, and our conversation of the other day has made me want to go to the mountain. Change of the moon is the best time to start out."

"Where would you go?" Flick asked.

"I thought of going a distance," Skunk replied. "I might," Skunk's idea grew as he thought, "go as far as Temple Mountain."

"We might go together, Skunk," Flickertail suggested. "Two of us might travel more safely than one."

"I would be honored, Mr. Flickertail," Skunk said. That was how the journey began.

It was a day of blue sky and sunshine when the two

small animals made their secret way out of the cellar window, down the hill from the Old Place and north, in which direction they surmised the mountain might be found. All was safe for them until they reached the road. Skunk's short legs took him briskly along. Although the Flickertail family had been ground squirrels in the beginning, they had learned to climb on the way east; so once in a while, when he oustripped Skunk, Flickertail took to a tree and looked ahead. They traveled for some time before they met with their first difficulty.

The teacher was on her way to the little red schoolhouse's vacation school, rattly-bang in her jeep. She was taking a couple of boys with her. There was fun at the vacation school—paints, games, crayons and stories.

"Watch out, Teacher," one boy warned. "There he goes, a squirrel with a yellow tail."

She searched her mind. She was the kindest of persons, tender to all small creatures. "There isn't a squirrel with a yellow tail anywhere," she said. "Gray, red, flying ones," she said firmly. "But they all have tails to match."

"We've seen it," the other boy said. "We boys plan to set a trap for it."

"Oh, I wouldn't do that," the teacher said vaguely, driving on. "The boys have been seeing things," she thought.

The two small travelers came out onto the road from the bushes where they had been hiding, but they had not gone far when they met old Mr. and Mrs. Mountain coming along from the post office. (In the village there lived Mountains, Hills, Brookses, Trees. They liked their country names and no one thought them odd. You could read their names written down in the Town Book.)

"Did you see it just now, hiding in the bushes?" Mr. Mountain said.

"What, Mr. Mountain?" she asked.

"That outlandish animal with the yellow tail," he explained. "Has the look of a squirrel but isn't. Ought to be run out of town."

Mrs. Mountain always agreed with her husband. "Now I think of it, perhaps I did see it," she said. They went on, and Flickertail and Skunk came out carefully and walked on.

"Is the mountain very much farther, Skunk?" Flickertail asked. His life had been so hard that he was nervous.

"You will be surprised," Skunk said, "how near our town is to one. It is not a very high mountain, but it will rise sharply when you get a bit farther on. The houses stop and the higher land begins. If we can make it before dark, all will be well, Mr. Flickertail."

Parson met them just then, but he had his nose in his sermon, pages of paper that he was reading to himself as he often did outdoors to practice for Sunday. The three met, but Flickertail and Skunk stayed bravely where they were on the road. They sensed that Parson would not do them harm. They were right. He only glanced at them. He must have seen the golden tail, but his thoughts were elsewhere. "A lovely day for a walk," he said to himself. "Why should not uncommon creatures be out?" He passed them, and the two went on cheerfully.

They reached the Common where boys were mowing the grass. The Common was a broad green space opposite the store and the church, where speeches were made and the band played. They stopped to watch. One boy sighted them.

"A skunk, and a squirrel with a wrong tail!" he shouted. "I'll get my rifle." He ran, the other boys following.

"Go on ahead, Mr. Flickertail," Skunk warned. "I'll fix things here and follow as soon as I can."

He was, as we know, a long-suffering creature, kind at heart. Once he had been foraging in the woodshed of the Old Place and he had got his head stuck in a partly empty jelly jar, cleaning it out. Bumping against walls and stairs, stuck in the jar, he had found his way toward the summer kitchen. There the grandmother had taken him into her lap. Slowly and carefully she had worked his head from the jar until he was free. "There you are, Sonny," she said. "Go outside and stay there. I can't promise to rescue you again." So Skunk had gone outside without harming the grandmother. But this was different. Action was called for.

Skunk sprayed the entire Common. When the boy with his rifle and the others came back they did not stay. Skunk hurriedly joined Flickertail, and they went on.

Well acquainted now, they enjoyed the pleasant weather

and talked over plans. On either side of the road, great bushes of wild pink roses bloomed. Farther on these were replaced by Juneberry bushes, from which they ate heartily. Skunk ate beetles and a small snake. Flickertail enjoyed green hazelnuts. "Have you any idea how you will spend the winter?" Flickertail asked him.

"Sleeping," Skunk replied, "but where remains to be seen. Our mountain is full of caves. I hope to find one small enough. There is nothing like a cave for comfortable living, cool in summer and warm in winter. I may not go with you to the top of the mountain, Mr. Flickertail, but I shall have you in mind."

"A cave sounds good, Skunk," he agreed. "I also may look for a cave."

Talking, traveling, their time passed. The sun warmed them and the trail became empty and safe. At last their way became somewhat slower, for the trail climbed, narrowed, and was rocky. They were now going up Temple Mountain. It arose before their astonished eyes in all its majesty. There is nothing in all the world so beautiful, so awesome as a mountain; lonely but friendly when you climb it, sweet smelling with pine trees, singing of rippling brooks, tasty with wild berries, telling stories if you have listening ears.

Flickertail and Skunk stopped, not for breath for they were not tired, but for the wonder of the mountain. Their troubles seemed gone. The mountain seemed to promise them a new and happier life.

"Well, here we are, Mr. Flickertail," Skunk said.

"All right, Skunk," Flickertail said, "but look who got here ahead of us."

Their peace of mind went. They were faced by the piercing beady eyes of a large brown bear.

4 · Settled In

THIS WAS Temple Mountain. They had come upon it so suddenly that all at once their past life seemed unreal. There were pink and white laurel blooming thickly, forests of fern, fiddlehead, lady fern already showing the tiny seeds that were said to make whoever ate them invisible to mortal eye, and lacy flowers of the wild parsnip.

When they looked over their shoulders, down below the towns were made up of tiny houses like those of a toy village and the streams were silver ribbons. It was a strange country, especially to Skunk, not quite so strange to Flicker-tail; and there ahead was Bear. Of the three, Bear seemed the most surprised.

Bear was sitting deep among some Juneberry bushes, eating. With both paws he was scooping off the berries and gulping pawfuls two at a time. His mouth dripped the blue juice. No one spoke at first, but when Bear had swallowed an impolite mouthful and saw that the odd couple of travelers

seemed too small to do him any harm, he asked in a gruff tone of voice, "Anything I can do for you two?"

"Please don't eat us," Flickertail said timidly. "We have come from the village. A mountain was spoken of as a good place on which to settle down for the winter."

Skunk now took courage. "Mr. Flickertail here," he explained, "has not been well treated in the village. His tail makes him freakish to some, a stranger to others."

Bear answered in his rumbling voice, standing up to his great bulk and backing away from them. "Eat you? I wouldn't think of it. These berries, with fish and the wild honey I get in old trees, are what I like to eat. That tail," he pointed one big paw at Flickertail, who had draped his golden tail over his arm and was brushing it as was his habit when he was nervous, "is a decoration. I would be proud to have such a tail myself. All my life I have had to get along with this stumpy tail."

"I would like to change with you, Bear," Flickertail said. "Down below in the village there is a well-known family of gray squirrels, the Nuttings, with whom I had hoped to board. But they will have nothing to do with me. In fact they do not seem to recognize me."

"I am in somewhat the same trouble," Skunk said. "I do no harm to anyone unless I am forced to."

"The same with me," rumbled Bear. "This mountain is infested with berry-pickers and fern-gatherers. Do I eat them? I do not. What are your plans for the coming days?" he asked in a neighborly way.

"We have come to live on the mountain." Flickertail said. "We left the village and here we are."

"Sound idea," Bear said. "I have lived here all my life, never bitten or eaten anybody. There is a lot of nonsense told about us bears. But I am somewhat in your position, unwanted but harmless. How do you plan to live?"

"A cave makes a good home," Skunk said. "I lived in a cave near the Old Place with my family, just above Second Brook. But my young grew up and left me."

"I myself live in a den under a cliff up yonder," Bear said. "It could not be cozier, warm in the winter, a shelter from storms, and quiet for my long sleep. These rocks are full of crannies and caves, some of them just the right size for small fellows like you two.

"There are certain things you must look to, though. Find a home near a brook. Look for such berries as checkerberries and twin berries for the winter. Nuts, too, are handy for storage. Ferns make good soft beds and those are plentiful as you go higher up. The woodpeckers speak of an early snowy winter this year. That is why I am eating heartily, to store up fat for my long sleep. I would advise you fellows to get busy at once on your home-hunting. You can spend the rest of the summer eating and storing your pantries. I would go along with you, but these berries are too tasty to leave." He waved a great paw to them as he sat down again in the berry patch.

They climbed on. "What a kindhearted person," Skunk said feelingly. "I shall always have a neighborly feeling after this for a bear."

"On the way east, I found bears harmless if you did not trouble them," Flickertail said. "Well, here we go."

Their trail was one of those called hairpin, straight and very narrow, then suddenly turning right around. At each turn the places below, small towns, streams, hills, became more and more distant. The pine trees became smaller, forests of ferns became thicker and taller. Tiny brooks sang over their pebbles, loud, rippling, high or sweet as their pebbles were large or small. The two travelers were glad of one another's company. Flickertail went back in his mind to the time when he was a ground squirrel and so kept to the trail, stayed close to Skunk.

In time they came to a mossy hillock with a doorway of rocks, hidden by bushes and with a stone ledge over the doorway to keep off the rain. Skunk explored it.

Flickertail could see that Skunk's feet were getting sore. He was not really a mountain climber. Skunk scratched his way inside the hole, then poked his head out. "It even smells like a home," he said, "of beetles and worms, dried grass and moss. Would you mind, Mr. Flickertail," he spoke in apology, "if I took this cave? I don't really see how I can climb any farther; having lived so long in the village, I am soft."

"The very place for you, Skunk, not too far from your old home and handy to me, for I do not expect to go much farther up myself. I have enjoyed your company. You may expect to have me drop in on you later after I get myself settled."

Skunk rolled into the cave and began scratching to get it into the kind of disorder he liked. His past way of life faded from his mind and he looked forward to a summer of peace and hearty meals. Flickertail gathered a bunch of soft grass to add to Skunk's bed. He gave a last look at the dizzying view below, the dangerous trail they had come up the mountain. Then he went on.

In a way he felt freer alone. Skunk had been a loyal friend and a pleasant traveling companion, but a bit plodding. Now Flickertail leaped onto trees, jumped from one

to another, took to earth when he wanted to feel the earth and make better progress. Above him the sky was so blue and hung so near that it seemed almost touchable. The ground was a green wilderness through which he pushed, and he began to follow a singing mountain stream from which he took cool sweet drinks. This was First Brook. As he traveled he looked for a home.

It came upon him all at once. Right in front of him, up high, at a turn in the trail with all below in the towns out of sight, it was there. This was a deeply set cranny in the rocks. It was wide enough for him to turn around in, it went so far into the rocks that it made an occupant invisible to anyone outside. Rock above it kept out storms and it had a door-stone in front. Flickertail went in to look it over.

Someone had lived there before. Jutting rocks made shelves on which were nutshells, which made Flickertail feel at home at once. Dried moss and leaves made a bed as comfortable as his bed in the back seat of Early Ford. Outside was First Brook, that gay little mountain stream. He could see silver trout darting in and out of the stones, and along the bank grew small shrubs of willow and alder that were tender and tasty. Flickertail wished he was a fisherman. Perhaps this was one of Bear's fishing holes. He would be glad to see Bear again.

Skunk had been right about the change of the moon being a good time to begin an adventure. Every night now the moon on the mountain grew larger and brighter. Flickertail settled down into his Cranny by bringing in fresh ferns and leaves, gathering a supply of hazelnuts, early but they would ripen, and filling his cheeks with juicy bits of bark for snacks. In the long bright evenings he sat on his door-stone and felt contented. He laid his golden tail on the stone beside him and looked with pride at its shining length. He knew that his tail was beautiful, if different from the general style of squirrels' tails. He thought of former days when the Flickertails wore their golden robes with black borders. He was sitting there, thinking, when he saw a strange sight.

An odd animal, somewhat larger than he, came cautiously down to the brook carrying quite a load of vegetables—

green beans, carrots, parsnips—and also short young twigs. His tail had black rings around it. His fur was thick, dark and dingy. He wore rings around his eyes which were like spectacles and made him look knowing. He peered cautiously in all directions, then set his load down on a flat stone on the bank of the brook. Flickertail silently went inside his Cranny and peeked out.

The newcomer began a strange task. One at a time, with paws that were shaped like human hands, he began washing his food—a bean dipped in the brook, taken out and scrubbed, then laid out to dry; an ear of corn shucked, dipped in the brook, taken out, scrubbed, and laid beside the bean. So this creature went on, dipping, washing, drying. It was all most peculiar.

How very peculiar, thought Flickertail; and that night he puzzled over it a long time before he went to sleep.

5 · Willie Takes a Trip

JUNE ROSES faded, the petals blew away and birds used them to line the nests of their young. New corn began to fill out, and there was talk in the village of a large crop of hay. So June sunned itself into July.

The Nutting family of squirrels who lived in the old Porter apple tree at the Old Place was busy, but in the back of their minds they had the same feeling of curiosity as before. Had they seen a strange squirrel in their neighborhood or had they not?

Miss Bushy Nutting was gathering a large pile of last fall's acorn cups that she would use for counting lessons when her classes for young squirrels opened in the fall. As she made plans to group them carefully in the children's sandbox in columns and tables, her mind was troubled. If she had never known of a creature like herself but partly yellow, was her mind slipping? Was there something lacking in her training as a teacher? She had been known for a long time as a smart teacher, up-to-date and strict. She could not bear to think that she might have made a mistake.

Mrs. Nutting did not think deeply except about her family. The Porter was so full of holes and crotches that every one of the family had a room with space left over. She busied herself gathering the summer leaves that were now right at hand. She also brought in other comforts, bits of soft new ferns, pillows of moss, and surprises in the form of leftover cracked corn from the chicken house. As Mrs. Nutting worked she came upon a new room in a crotch of the tree, empty. It occurred to her that she would like to furnish it, but for whom? Perhaps for the stranger.

"Mr. Nutting would not approve," she thought. "He says there is no such creature as a squirrel wearing yellow."

Mr. Nutting went about his business as head of the family, climbing oak trees to see how the new acorns were coming along, slipping in and out of cornfields to inspect the crops, stuffing his cheeks with new peas. He refused to remember that once, a long while back, he had met a squirrel like himself but having a flowing yellow tail. It was not true. His first name was Hickory, which meant he was hard-headed.

As for Grandpa Nutting, old and somewhat witless, he tottered about the lanes admiring the flowing blooms of the goldenrod that was early this year, looking at his mangy gray tail and thinking how beautiful a one the goldenrod would make. Miss Bushy followed him about, seeing that no harm came to him. "Let him dream," she told the others.

"It is all he can do now. Of course he is mistaken about that stranger we thought we saw."

Willie S. almost never left the attic and the books. He was the thoughtful one of the family. Whether he was better educated, or all the leather-bound books he chewed had given him a more active brain, was not known. He thought all the time and hard about the golden creature he had glimpsed; was it real or his fancy? He could not sleep, in the castoff mattress which was his bed in the attic, for thinking. When he crept out the attic window and along the flagpole to the Porter, he looked wild-eyed. Finally he decided to take steps.

It was Mrs. Nutting who made the discovery. Willie S. was her only son. As a small ball of gray fur she had cuddled him in his baby days. She had showed him low branches for jumping among. She did not completely understand him now that he had become so bookish, but she loved him.

"Willie S. is gone," Mrs. Nutting said one day. "I climbed up and looked in the attic window. He isn't there."

July was one of the most important months in the entire year in the village, the month of the Ladies Aid Fair. This was because the Ladies Aid always had some good cause for which it needed money. Also it was a gay occasion. Weather permitting, the fair was held on the Common, green and sightly in its smooth turf. The center of the Common was reserved for the pony rides; for ten cents a child could ride twice around. All around the edge of the Common were tables of exciting things for sale—odds and ends that some families did not want but other families did, food such as cookies and pies and fudge, painted wooden animals and dolls, bouquets of blue cornflowers, marigolds and zinnias, plants ready for setting out in the gardens, fresh vegetables, pot holders of figured cloth. A big bag of ten-cent grabs was popular. And the aprons!

Although somewhat out of fashion, the village ladies wore aprons almost all day. A long line was strung from two trees and on this, hung by clothespins, were the aprons that were for sale. Ruffled aprons; aprons with designs of apples, flowers, checks and stripes; aprons with strings; aprons with bibs; aprons with big pockets. These aprons waved in the breeze as if they were kitchen flags. They were admired by young and old. By sundown every apron would be sold.

The Common was crowded with village people wearing their prettiest summer dresses. The older people rested on benches provided for them; the children got underfoot but no one minded, for was this not the great Fair Day! Lemonade was drunk and hot dogs were eaten. The sun shone hot and bright. Money passed hands. It was all as usual until something happened that was quite out of the ordinary.

Willie S. started out from the Old Place, somewhat confused by the sunshine after the dimness of the attic. He crossed the back lawn, followed the bank of Second Brook until it trickled into the village, then he climbed trees until he was out of sight of everything familiar. He traveled until he came to a thicket of woods. Going through, he suddenly came upon a brilliant scene. Willie Nutting had come to the Ladies Aid Fair!

Under ordinary circumstances so many grownups and children would have interested Willie. Now, the strange scene, the tables of colored wares, the crowd, the ponies went to his head. He lost his wits completely. He fell out of a tree smack into the large pocket of one of the aprons strung on the line beneath the tree. All at once an apron, its strings loose and flying, fell down onto the grass and dashed around the Common.

A crowd of boys and girls followed the traveling apron, too awed to touch it. This could have gone on indefinitely had not Willie managed to get out of the pocket, more confused than before. He made a great jump and landed on the food table, right in the middle of a molasses pie.

The village was given to wearing aprons. It was also fond of eating pie. The food table was richly spread with apple, custard, cherry, lemon-meringue and blueberry pies. But of all these, a molasses pie is the stickiest and the worst one Willie could have selected to fall into. A ring of laughing children watched him try to get out. The lady in charge of the food table was afraid to touch him. He pulled out one foot only to stick in another. His fur became sticky with molasses. When at last he got himself loose he leaped without any sense of direction into the bag of grabs.

For ten cents one dipped into the bag and took out a grab; but no one felt like dipping into the bag that was filled to the top with wrapped whistles, dolls, small airplanes, tiny automobiles and such like, for they had a notion that squirrels bite. Poor Willie, who never bit anybody! The pony rides stopped. Other sales stopped. How long Willie struggled among the packages he never afterward could remember. At last the lady in charge of the grabs tipped the bag and Willie was loose. Thickly coated with molasses, with colored paper sticking to his fur, Willie ran as he had never run before to the shelter of trees that stood in the back of the Common. Lost in their surprise as they were, no one ventured to follow him. Alone there in the woods, Willie, worn out, fell into Second Brook.

When Mrs. Nutting discovered Willie's absence she started out to find him. She was timid by nature, and this was a brave act on her part. She had nothing to guide her until she crossed the lawn and came to his footprints along the bank of Second Brook. These she followed, and when the water grew shallower bits of bark and twigs he had left made a trail that guided her. She almost never went anywhere so she found the going hard. Once she had a glimpse of a woodchuck, fat and prowling, out hunting in farmers' lands for new green beans. She wondered if this were the strange yellowish creature that had been seen back home. She decided no. Mr. Nutting would have spoken of it. The next day she came upon Willie.

He lay on the edge of Second Brook, almost indistinguishable as a squirrel. The water and sand of the brook, although he had gotten out easily, had made him look worse. And he had no desire to clean himself.

"Willie!" She was shocked. "What happened?"

"Fair . . . aprons . . . pie . . ." he stopped. Even a squirrel with a larger brain than Mrs. Nutting's would have been hard pressed to understand what Willie was trying to explain. She patted him. "There, there, son, don't strain yourself talking. I can see that you have had a hard time. But whatever brought you here?"

"I was looking for the golden squirrel," Willie said. "I wanted to find out for myself if it was real. No book in the attic spoke of such an animal, so I started out to look for it."

"And did you find out?"

"No," he told her. "I only got into trouble."

"Well, just let it pass," she tried to comfort him. "We will go home and a few days rolling on the warm grass will take all this stuff off you. You really did a brave thing, Willie. Your father will be proud of you."

He pulled himself up from the bank where he was stuck. He was thankful to be with his mother. Walking and jumping a safe distance apart so that none of the stickiness would come off on to Mrs. Nutting, they started in the direction of home. From time to time Willie muttered, "There isn't such an animal. There is *not!*" It seemed to give him a certain satisfaction in spite of the danger he had gone through.

6 · *Little Beaver's Party*

FLICKERTAIL SAT on the door-stone of his new home, the Cranny, combing and brushing his tail. His comb was a small hemlock cone, his brush a pine cone. Up and down, brush, up and down, brush. With each stroke the hairs of his tail sprang to life, became more glossy and bright. He viewed his mountain home, thinking how well suited it was to his needs, how pleasant a place to spend his days. The inside of the Cranny he had furnished with fresh moss rugs, and the shelves in the rock held an ample store of food for the fall and winter, when he expected to spend a large part of his time sleeping. No longer did he fear being chased. He had already made a few friends. Bear had called once, his jaws dripping with honey from a tree that held a wild-bees' nest. At night the full moon was his lamp, and if it rained the Cranny, deep and snug, made music. Mountain life was a good life he said to himself.

As he was being thankful, something dropped beside Flickertail on the door-stone. Wonderful! It was a kernel of ripe corn. He ate it. Down dropped another. He looked up into the branches of a pine tree that grew beside the Cranny. There he saw an odd face wearing black-rimmed spectacles. A black-ringed tail hung down. There sat Coon, whom Flickertail had seen washing his food in the clear water of First Brook. With his plump humanlike hands Coon held an ear of green corn. He was shucking it and gnawing off kernels, just as a person would. Seeing Flickertail, Coon chuckled.

"Surprised you, didn't I?" he said. "I took a trip down the mountain and brought back all the corn I could carry. Green corn is at its best now, full in the ear and sweet." He slipped nimbly down the tree and joined Flickertail.

"Neighbor," he said, "are you comfortable, well settled in? Coon is my name."

"Could not be more comfortable," Flickertail replied.

Coon sat down. "Nothing better than mountain living," he said. "I used to be a tame coon, down below, in town. But the life was too restricted. I ran away."

"You don't say," Flickertail said. "Where did you go?"

"Just around the village, stopping at back doors for hand-outs. But when some persons saw me, they were scared. I'm not a handsome fellow, scraggly and walking on two legs sometimes; then these big spectacles and the rings on my tail give me the look of a tramp."

"I can well understand," Flickertail replied, spreading his golden fluffy tail. "It is a trial to look different."

"Where did you get that tail?" Coon asked.

"It runs in the family," Flickertail explained. "We used to have golden cloaks with black borders until we began coming out here from the West. Now our tails, when they are seen, are held against us."

They sat there not speaking for a while, just being mountain happy. Then Coon spoke. "There is a party farther up the trail this afternoon," Coon said. "I think you might like to attend. Little Beaver got caught in a trap. Dreadful things, those traps! He hurt his leg and was several days getting home to the family lodge. Now Beaver is giving him a party. You might enjoy it, but I don't know." He looked at Flickertail. "Beaver might resent you. You see he has a broad flat tail that he uses for spreading mud. It is useful but nothing to be proud of." He thought. Then, "Why not wash your tail?" he suggested.

Flicktertail was ready to try anything, having been through so much trouble. He agreed and spread his tail widely on a flat stone on the bank of First Brook. Coon began dipping up water with his hands, dripping it on Flickertail's tail and scrubbing. Scrub, scrub, rinse, rinse. More water. Scrub, scrub, rinse, rinse. But the tail, so well combed and brushed of the chaff of the barn at the Old Place and the dust of town and mountain, only became more bright, more golden. The warm air dried it, and it flashed in the bright noon sun.

Coon gave up. "Fast color," he said. "Well, we might risk

going to the party. Beaver may be in a good mood. All his young have left to build their own lodges, and Little Beaver is his favorite. I'll call for you later."

They had an early lunch of the rest of the green corn generously given by Coon. Then they started out, Coon a tall shabby person but most friendly, Flickertail's tail a floating feather curled over his back.

"If you don't mind, Flickertail, we will go cautiously," Coon said. "I have to watch for traps. Baked coon is a delicacy among two-leggers."

"I have troubles, too, but different," Flickertail said. "I seem to be invisible to some; others chase me. Where do you live, Coon?"

"Here and there," Coon replied. "Mostly in hollow trees during the daytime, in treetops at night. My eyes shine red in the evening, which is a help to hunters. This way. We follow the stream going toward the north."

Beaver's place came upon them suddenly—a well-made dam of stones and mud that made a pond, a blue sheet of water, and on the beach his lodge with mud-plastered walls and boughs laid over to hide it.

"What's that?" Flickertail pointed to a branch of laurel leaves floating all alone on the surface of the water.

"Beaver is underwater," Coon told him. "If you look sharp you will see his nose. He is making a new bed for Little Beaver to get well on. He misses his family, but that is what happens nowadays. You bring up your children and off they go to build their own lodges. Back and forth over his pond, back and forth Beaver has been going and coming, fetching soft sprigs of laurel, making Little Beaver a wide soft bed to rest his hurt leg on."

They peered from beneath a thicket of young pine trees for some time until Beaver disappeared in the door of the lodge, bringing his last load of branches of laurel.

"Soon now," Coon said, "the party will begin. I doubt if any of his family will swim back for the party, but his neighbors are bound to drop in."

Coon picked a bunch of mint that grew along the bank. "It will be a tonic for Little Beaver," he explained. Flickertail gathered some juicy willow twigs for Little Beaver to gnaw. Then they went stealthily along the edge of the pond until they came out on top of the beavers' lodge. There, through openings in the roof of the lodge, they peeked down in. They were still undecided as to their welcome. The inside of the lodge, well plastered with mud, was neat, cool and dry. Little Beaver, a sharp-eyed youngster of silky brown fur, lay with his wounded leg on a pillow of pink

laurel blossoms. His father sat beside him patting the little
fellow from time to time. That is, until he happened to look
up and saw four eyes at the roof. He went over to the door.

"Come in!" he said. "Our party will begin at any moment."
Then, looking in surprise at Flickertail, he said, "Come in,
stranger. What a handsome fellow! Come right in. Wonder-

ful!" They scrambled down. "Our neighbor, Flickertail,"
Coon introduced him.

"No one ever before spoke of me as handsome," Flickertail told Beaver. "I am unused to such praise."

"But you are a fine-looking fellow," Beaver repeated. "I
wish I had a golden tail, but I am hard-working, born this
way." He led the way to the entrance of his lodge.

The party began with music. Seated on stones in First Brook, several frogs sounded their bass drums. Boom. Boom. Boom. Wild ducks who had lighted on the bank gave shrill cries. Woodpeckers tapped on the trees and sounded like tap dancers. Bluejays dropped their bell tones just when the music needed it. More frogs, not stopping for breath, kept them all going in a kind of mountain jazz.

"Stand away from the door so Little Beaver can look out," Beaver told his guests. "Help yourselves to refreshments." He had a fine feast of tender twigs, clover and twinberries for them. Little Beaver moved his leg, tried to step with it. The excitement was already helping him. The music attracted a larger company. Cranes flew down from farther up the mountain and did their two-legged dance on the bank of the pond. Grasshoppers and early crickets added

their shrill songs whenever they could get in a note. A wood thrush in the top of an old pine tree played his flute earlier in the day than was his wont. A mountain owl, awakened by the music, hooted hoarsely, rivaling the drums of the frogs.

"I never heard anything as exciting as this," Flickertail told Coon. "This is a new experience for me."

"When we give a party here on the mountain, it *is* a party," Coon boasted. "Beaver is as happy as you. He hopes Little Beaver will stay at home now and be a comfort to him."

In the meantime Beaver was busy, going out and in, gathering more young twigs to gnaw, armfuls of fresh clover and pitcher plants full to the brim with cool pond water. Time meant nothing to them. When they became tired of the music, some of the players came into the lodge. The bullfrogs did a clumsy, hopping dance to amuse Little Beaver.

Coon did his share of the entertaining. He stood on his head. He turned somersaults. His shabby clothes seemed only to add to his effect. He even tossed twigs in the air and caught them in his mouth. He was a success. Flickertail discovered that he could sing, short, clear notes that added to the dance. Birds pattering their feet could be heard on the roof. A cricket came in to say he would live in the lodge for the rest of the season if his chirping would be of any comfort to Little Beaver. No one missed the rest of the Beaver family, knowing they were about their business of being beavers. Mother Beaver was off somewhere plastering, but would return.

At one moment of the party, a gruff voice could be heard on the bank of the pond. Coon went out and returned with a dripping wild-honey comb. "From Bear," he explained.

"His regrets that he is too big to come to the party in person."

Everybody except the smaller ones and those who did not eat sweets went to it and became unbelievably sticky. Beaver looked out his door. "No one need hurry," he said, "but the primroses are closing. And Little Beaver needs his rest. Thank you all, especially you," he pointed to Flickertail, "for coming and doing so much to make the party a success."

One by one they left; Coon and Flickertail were the last to go. They took their long way home at last, lighted by fireflies.

"A fine time," Flickertail told Coon at the door of the Cranny. "Thank you for taking me, Coon. I wish you would come in and spend the night."

"Unsafe," Coon said. "My eyes are too bright. But I shall be seeing you." He tramped off, looking in the dusk more than ever like a vagabond. Flickertail watched him until he was only a shadow, then not even that. He went thankfully inside the Cranny. Mountaineers have warm hearts, he thought, as he curled his tail around him and settled down for the night.

7 · *The White Deer*

THIS WAS the hour that Flickertail liked best, twilight of a summer day. Dew fell on the wild roses, the primroses and honeysuckles that bloomed around his Cranny filling the air with their perfume. Birds who had been flying toward the top of the mountain in the sunshine now came toward their home nests, twittering a good night. The ferns that grew in Flickertail's own special bracken near his door-stone now sent out a spicy smell. His earth seemed more mysterious as twilight fell. Not having anyone to send him to bed, he went for a short walk among the ferns. They were wide-spreading, taller than he—the Christmas ferns were as tall as trees to Flickertail, the fiddlehead ferns with their musical shape on which it was said the spirits of the mountain played on Allhallows Eve, the dainty maidenhair ferns that were favorites of fairies, the dagger ferns with which elves practiced fencing. All these forms, damp and dewy, pleased Flickertail. The ground was cool to his feet, and his nose tickled.

It was again the change of the moon which now rose above him, vast and orange-colored. Instead of a yellow glow, the moonlight shone white. It shone on his land with a brilliance that was brighter than day. It dazzled him, and he snuggled among the taller ferns. Suddenly he saw a wonder. Never in all his adventuresome life had he seen anything so awesome. Flickertail trembled with fear. Beside him among the ferns, nosing about, was an enormous four-footed creature, white as the moonlight, stepping on light hoofs, tossing a proud antlered head, then bowing to the silvery earth. Then this white creature would nibble a fern for which it seëmed to have been searching.

Flickertail had not really been afraid of Bear. Bear had seemed to him almost from his first glimpse a friendly old blundering jokester, which he was. This pale stranger was different, like a visitor from another world. It moved among ferns, tossed its head toward the vast light of the full moon that now seemed to rest on the mountain top, then stepped out on to the green moss before Flickertail's door-stone and lifted its hoofs in a stately dance. Back and forth, up and down as gracefully as a pine tree moves in a summer breeze, the white creature danced alone with grace. Its great head was held high, its body shone as pale as silver. Flickertail crept out of the bracken and into his Cranny.

Flickertail had a comfortable bed. He had made rolls of dried grass, carefully measured and fitted together, to spread in a corner of the Cranny. Lying there with the night perfume and the quiet—for the birds were now still—he slept.

In the morning he decided that the moonlight, the enchanted mountain, had given him a dream. So when he heard a loud scratching outside, he called cheerfully, "Come in. Come right in." In lumbered Skunk, whom he had not seen in all this time.

"Well, stranger," he hailed Skunk. "How are you? Did you think I had forgotten you?"

Skunk helped himself to a breakfast of berries. "Not at all, Mr. Flick," he said. "It took me a while to dig out just the burrow I wanted. Then I took a walk down the mountain and met a roadside skunk and got some news about our old home."

"I have news, too, Skunk," Flickertail began, but Skunk appeared not to hear. He went right on. "Willie Nutting actually went on a trip to look you up, but he fell into the Ladies Aid Fair and got himself messed up."

"Ladies Aid Fair?"

This was another mystery to Flickertail, but Skunk just then saw Beaver making his slippery way toward the Cranny. "There is a beaver," he exclaimed. "I have not seen one in years. I must look at his lodge. It might be a pleasant place for the winter. Glad to have seen you, Mr. Flick. Be seeing you again." Skunk was off.

Beaver was less at home on land than in the water. He shook himself dry as he slithered into the Cranny. "I was worried about you," he said. "It was a good party, wasn't it?"

"Couldn't have been better, Beaver. And how is Little Beaver?"

"Up and around," Beaver said. "His mother came home, and that helped him. She takes these trips once in a while to see how the rest of our family is getting along, but she always comes back. And you, neighbor?"

Flickertail started again telling about the night before. "It is the change of the moon," he said. "I was excited by the moonlight out there. It was a different world. Everything was white and shining. I didn't want to go to bed, so I went out to see what I could see. I was in among the ferns out there." He pointed to the ferns beyond his door-stone. "All at once a strange four-footed creature, all white, was there beside me, tall and eating ferns...." He was going to tell the entire story when Beaver interrupted him. "Well, well. And did you eat any ferns?"

"Not a nibble," Flickertail said. "To tell the truth I was too scared. You know, the white night, the tall animal, and the big moon ready to drop on me."

"What I want to know," Beaver said, paying slight attention to the story, "is did you eat any ferns?"

"Not a frond," Flickertail answered. "I had no appetite at the time."

"Good!" Beaver said. "Stick to your usual meals, I always say. Now I might be tempted to go down some night for supper with Skunk but it wouldn't agree with me. Down below they have a snack cabin for mountain climbers and one finds bits of sandwiches and the like. I know enough to avoid strange foods. Take my advice and be careful of your diet." Beaver started home.

No one seemed interested in his experience of the night before. Flickertail more and more looked upon his moonlit vision as a dream. It was cloudy for a few nights, and Flickertail stayed inside. The days were foggy, but the moon shone at last. As he was out gathering bundles of hay, down at his feet dropped a bunch of tasty string beans. Looking up, he saw the big gleaming black spectacles of Coon in a tree. Coon, grinning, slid down, more green stuff in his arms.

"Hi, neighbor," he said. "I have had you in mind, if I haven't called. It is getting late for string beans, and while the two-leggers are away haying I get into the gardens. Then I must wash and rinse everything I bring home. Always wash *and* rinse, I say. How goes it with you?"

Rough-and-ready Coon looked dependable. Flickertail enjoyed a few beans and then decided he would tell Coon about his dream. "Coon, is there a white ghost on this mountain, a ghost who has four legs, antlers, and is around at night now the moon has changed and shines full?"

Coon's forehead wrinkled, giving him the appearance of a deep thinker.

"The moon was out, and I couldn't sleep," Flickertail said. "I was taking a walk among my ferns and a great white four-legged creature..."

Coon dropped from the tree, folded his hands over his eyes as if in a great light. "Four-legged? White? With great silvery antlers? It was nosing about in the bracken?" Coon trembled as he spoke. Then he came closer to Flickertail. "Flick," he said, pointing with his small hands toward the top of the mountain, "You have been given a vision. Have you spoken to anybody of this?"

"Only to Skunk and Beaver," Flickertail said. "They gave me little heed."

"Both, plodding men with little imagination," Coon said. "They would never have seen what you did."

"What did I see, Coon?"

"The White Deer of the mountain, looking for the seeds of the lady fern. Eating this fern seed, he makes himself invisible. Once..."

"What? Go on," Flickertail begged.

"It was the year I gave up being a tame Coon. I lived alone up here and had made very few friends. It was cold, and I stayed in a hollow tree. Christmas Eve came. Down in the village we had hung up stockings and had lighted candles in the windows. Two-leggers came up the mountain and cut evergreens to trim the houses. Christmas Eve was quiet and still."

"What happened?" Flickertail wanted to know. Coon seemed almost loath to speak.

"The White Deer came, with a bright star on its forehead, between the antlers. I stayed in my tree, but looked outside. The star made a trail of silver, and that lighted the earth. Wherever it stepped spring flowers bloomed. When it raised its head the birds of spring flew back and sang. There was a robin staying with us for the winter because of a broken wing. It flew ahead of the White Deer, strong and singing again. All this, Flick, I saw."

"You think...?" Flickertail could hardly speak for excitement.

"I don't think. I know." Coon looked seriously through his spectacles. He even examined the thicket of ferns, noting where hoofs had left imprints in the damp earth. He returned to Flickertail's door-stone. "You saw the White Deer,

Flick." He would have looked pale if his natural expression had not been so dingy. "It is seldom seen, and only by very special mountaineers. He searches for the seed of the lady fern. He has need of being invisible. Later, after Christmas, I made inquiries. The White Deer is unseen except by special people with special eyesight. Birds that fall out of nests, wounded, orphaned fawns, creatures like these the White Deer succors. That Christmas night I found fresh vegetables at the doors of my hollow tree, although the gardens were under snow."

Flickertail's bright eyes were wide with wonder. "You surprise me, Coon. I have never thought of myself as anyone special."

"Believe me, Flick, you must be." Coon gathered up the rest of his beans and started for First Brook. He moved slowly, thinking of Flick as a very special neighbor indeed.

As for Flickertail, he became so absent-minded that he forgot to make his bed. He washed his tail in the brook and then gave it a thorough brushing. Was there, he wondered, anything admirable about him? The mountain was kind to him, but he could not forget the Nuttings down below who did not see, or worse, denied him. He waited and watched all that moon for the White Deer but he did not see it again.

8 · *Bushy Travels*

MISS BUSHY NUTTING felt a strong urge to go somewhere. The summer vacation had not given her much of a change. She had busied herself collecting acorn cups for counting lessons when her school opened, and small twigs with which her pupils could learn to write their letters in the sandbox. These duties were now finished. She had also Grandpa Nutting to care for. He lived with her at the far end of the great back lawn under the oak trees. He had given up gathering nuts. This season he had a habit of wandering off, losing himself in the fields of goldenrod that was blooming early, examining the feathery golden stalks, comparing them with his mangy gray tail.

Guiding him home, Bushy would say, "It is of no use, Grandpa. Goldenrod would not make you a durable tail even if there was any way of attaching it. There is no such person as a yellow squirrel that some of us thought we saw." But Grandpa went on exploring. These cares and thinking about the wild young squirrels, whom she would have to cope with before too long, gave Bushy her urge to travel before the school term began. She climbed the Porter apple tree at an early hour one day when it was likely to be deserted. Mr. Hickory Nutting was off looking for food. Mrs. Nutting was out of sight, busy with housekeeping. Bushy leaped from a bough of the tree to the flagpole, her only way of getting inside the house. She had never been inside and thought it would be a good starting place.

Crawling along the flagpole, she could have been a circus trapeze walker, or a telephone repairman. Below, the earth seemed lost to her. Above, the house loomed large. She was amazed at Willie's intrepid trips to and fro so often. She made it, and crawled in through the open window, looking for Willie, who was seldom seen now. Remembering the Ladies Aid Fair, he felt safer in the attic.

"Willie. Willie S." Bushy called.

A small rustling gave a hint of his whereabouts. Willie peered out from a box of old letters that he was chewing up to make himself a new bed. "Why, Aunt Bush," Willie exclaimed, "what brings you here?"

The attic was a pleasant litter. A spinning wheel. A big white plaster mold on which in far-back days they fashioned straw and silk bonnets. A bandbox covered with flowered paper to hold a bonnet. Books. Books! These gave special interest to the attic.

"The need of a trip," she explained. "Also, I have not forgotten our discussion a while back about a stranger among us. I want to find out the truth of the matter."

"Don't do it," Willie warned, coming out from his mess

of papers, still somewhat draggled. "Remember, I took a trip and had nothing but trouble. I am thinking of giving up books, Aunt Bushy, and trying to be more practical. I do hope you will not leave us."

"I have decided," Bushy said.

"Do give it thought, then," Willie said. "I am younger than you and have tried it."

"I have made up my mind." Bushy spoke firmly.

"I would make a nest for you up here." Willie became

firm too. "I assure you a squirrel could find a much worse place for the winter than an attic, safe and interesting too. Look here." Willie became the guide of a museum. He jumped out of the chest and opened-the large bandbox. "Here there was a beautiful flowered straw bonnet with purple velvet ribbon strings, made on this plaster bonnet mold. However, I can show you only the pieces. The mice ate it."

"You don't say!" Bushy was polite but not interested.

"Here," Willie went on, "is the spinning wheel." He leaped onto it and began whirling the wheel round and round dizzily. It spun and hummed as if it were still in use.

"I am going away for a journey." Bushy spoke her last word.

"Well then, go, Aunt Bushy," he said, "but don't blame me if you get into trouble. All the books I have read up here did not save me.

"Take the north stairway behind those shelves of travel books. They are plainly marked *Travel*," he told her. "Once on the bedroom floor take the staircase down to the kitchen. There you may find a few cracker crumbs and rice kernels if the mice have not cleaned out the pantry. If you don't come home, Aunt Bushy, I shall miss you."

She made her way cautiously through the litter of the attic—old trunks, old clothes to dress up in, various things like brass beds and cracked china, guns and swords, a war helmet and breastplate and such. She found the furniture below wrapped in covers. The field mice were away now, the haying having called them. This was their harvest. They ate green seeds and made themselves burrows in the gleaning left from the mowing. She entered the great space of the barn.

The barn was large and exciting. It had stood for years across the road where it had shut off the view of the mountain. Then the family had moved it and fastened it to the side of the house, with a door into it from the summer kitchen, so one could go in and out without getting into the weather. Not having any longer a cow or a horse, they had given it over to the children and cars. It was wonderful— it had two stories, with stalls; there were a wheelbarrow, a cart made of orchard field boxes and castoff wheels, a grindstone for sharpening jackknives, an old croquet set, still good, homemade bows and arrows and a target, an old chest of drawers full of games, a long ping-pong table for playing the games. Rainy days were happy days there for the children. Also, Early Ford stayed there. It was understandable that Bushy had never seen the barn. She was once and always a teacher and a homebody.

Living as she always had, off the road, Bushy seldom saw a car. If she did see one when visiting her family in the Porter tree, she looked the other way, finding it strange and fearsome. Now, seeing the huge body of Early Ford, close and unknown, Bushy felt that adventure had come right into her life. She felt a new courage. Perhaps, she thought, here was her trip right at hand. She sniffed the tires, scratched the paint, darted in under the wheels, became completely rash. Early Ford looked reliable and ready, so to speak, waiting for her. She did not question why a door was open. Miss Bushy climbed a tire and leaped inside.

Bushy was reflected in the mirror, an odd little figure. She had no idea that Early Ford would not start, taking her for the journey she wanted, out into the world to solve the mystery of the phantom squirrel the Nutting family was so troubled about. But since Early Ford stood there, unmoving and enormous, Bushy began exploring.

She climbed and scratched. She found the hollow in the back seat that had been Flickertail's winter nest. It was still soft and snug. She curled herself up in it, finding it a perfect fit. Scrabbling about on the floor, she came upon a surprise— some nutshells completely cleaned of the meat. This gave Bushy more assurance that in some odd way this mammoth thing had come into being for her use. Willie did not, she felt, in spite of his wide reading in the attic, know every- thing. Bushy scrabbled around more actively, stirring up dust and trying to attract the attention of this great machine. She jumped over onto the front seat.

Bushy climbed about the front seat, inspecting every- thing. Then she jumped onto the steering wheel, landing exactly on the horn.

Early Ford honked.

This was so unexpected by Bushy, not being squirrel talk as she had known it, that she got into a panic. She leaped out, got tangled in an old tennis net in the barn, caught her feet in the swing rope, lost her way, and scrambled up into the hayloft instead of going outdoors to the Porter. She finally got home to the oak trees with her heart beating until it choked her. There Grandpa Nutting had missed her and as usual had gotten into mischief. She had persuaded him to begin burying nuts early, which he had started to do; but he was now digging them up, at least those he could find, and was busily eating them. Acorns were falling early, a sign of a hard winter.

"Grandpa, what shall I do with you," Bushy chattered. She began shaking and brushing herself to remove the dust of the barn. It was then that she made the discovery. In her fur, Bushy found a number of long, soft, golden hairs!

There was only one explanation. Whoever it was, whatever sign she had happened on, someone had been there in the barn before her—someone strange and golden. Willie seldom left his attic. Mrs. Nutting was always busy housekeeping. Hickory Nutting was avoiding any talk about any unusual squirrel. The mice were out in the hayfield, stuffing themselves on grass seeds. All this thought, Bushy knew, was beside the point, for no one in the neighborhood had yellow fur.

9 · *Fire on the Mountain*

COON HAD a hobby. He collected glassware. This hobby
had started when he lived in town trying to be a tame coon.

His town family had given him unwashed glass jars from
which, with his little hands, he scraped and ate such treats
as strawberry jam, peanut butter and cheese. Then, as a
tramp coon begging at back doors, he had looked for such
jars but seldom found one. On the mountain, picknickers
sometimes left broken glass that Coon eagerly picked up,
washed when he was washing his food and laid about where
he could enjoy looking at it. His treasures were a green glass
pickle bottle through which he sometimes looked, like a
ship's captain with a spyglass, a piece of a cracked red glass
saucer, a yellow tumbler somewhat chipped, a pink mug
also cracked and such like. When he had nothing else to
do Coon would make the rounds of the collection of glassware and, holding the pieces up to his spectacles, look
through them. The colors gave an entirely different look to
his world, red grass, a green sky and yellow trees. This was

one of his simple pleasures. He had not mentioned his collection to Flicketail, not being sure that Flickertail would appreciate it.

But the red glass saucer was his favorite. He felt that its bright outlook on their earth and sky should be shared. He decided to surprise Flickertail. One sunny hot day, when he had seen Flickertail start out toward the Beavers' lodge, Coon rubbed the red glass until it shone and then crept over to the Cranny and laid it near the door-stone. He thought of the pleasure it would be to show Flickertail the magic qualities of the colored glass, how, looking through it, he could see a new world. He might even give it to Flickertail if he showed interest in it.

Now that midsummer was past and the time of Indian summer drawing near, the days were blazing hot at noon. That was mountain weather—cool enough to snuggle down beneath leaves or dig a deeper burrow for the nights, scorching hot if you wore fur in the daytime. It was a time to enjoy the weather, to take long walks, and eat large meals to lay on the fat for the long winter's sleep. After he had left his surprise for Flickertail, Coon started out to find some last ears of corn that could be shucked and kept stored for later meals. So the Cranny was alone for a while. The sun rose higher as noon came. It shone like a furnace on the dry grass Flickertail kept in small piles around his home, in case a neighbor came for the night and needed another pillow. It shone on the piece of red glass, hotter and hotter.

When Flickertail came home from his call on the Beavers, he did not see the glass because a narrow trail of smoke arose from the grass around it. Flickertail had seen bonfires in his past travels. He scampered toward First Brook. His voice was a frightened chatter.

"Coon, Coon," he called. "Run. The mountain's on fire."

Coon came at a brisk trot. "What's this? What's the matter, Flick?" he called. Then he saw. He had no idea what to do. But Flickertail knew. "Crawl into the very back of my Cranny," he warned. "Stay there! It is deep and you will be safe. I'm off to warn the mountain. This is the start of a forest fire."

Already tiny bursts of flame, no larger than a candle flame, pierced the smoke from the pile of dried grass that had taken fire from the hot glass. Coon followed his advice, and soon only the last ring of his tail could be seen in the depths of the Cranny. Flickertail leaped over the burning grass and ran to the waterside.

"Fire on the mountain! Swim, Beavers, swim!" Flickertail called. The three beavers dived into their pond.

Some frogs jumped up onto the bank. Flickertail called to them. "Fire on the mountain! Dive, Frogs. Dive!" The frogs ducked into the water beneath some weeds where they would be safe.

Flickertail leaped on, as fast as the wind which was rising and fanning the sparks of the fire into brighter flashes. That was the way of a forest fire, slow in starting, then growing with the lightest breeze until it was beyond checking. He ran through the smoke to see if Coon had taken shelter. Apparently he had, for not even the tip of his tail showed now. Then Flickertail started down the mountain. He had to make haste, for the smoke choked him. The fire still was mainly smoke. At a rabbit's burrow, he chattered hoarsely.

"Fire on the mountain. Run, Rabbit, run!"

At other burrows, holes in the hollow trees, and tall crags where birds like owls, crows and hawks nested, Flickertail called, "Fire on the mountain! Fly, Birds, fly! The birds soared high and safe, but the leaves of the trees were beginning to scorch in the heat.

As Flickertail dashed on down the mountain trail, he was followed by a line of running, leaping animals and wild fowl. More rabbits. Fat, plodding woodchucks, quill pigs, foxes, badgers, woodcocks, quail, pheasants, the belled turkey tinkling along and followed by his hens. Owls in the treetops opened sleepy eyes and hooted. To one and all, Flickertail called, "Fire on the mountain! Run, run, run!"

The smoke was now too dense for him to see clearly. His feet were getting too hot for comfort. It was when he felt almost too tired to go on that he heard a voice he knew.

"Honk! Honk! Honk!" Amazing, so far away from home, but there was Early Ford lumbering up the mountain. He seemed to be saying, "All is under control, Flick, my boy." He was bringing up the village fire department.

Someone from the village had seen the crowd of little animals fleeing down the mountain trail, led by the squirrel with the shining tail. The unaccustomed sight had led to the discovery of smoke on the mountain. The village did not have a regular fire department, but it had a brigade that served about as well. The back of the car was full of burlap potato sacks that would be soaked in First Brook and used to beat out the blaze. Behind came the teacher's jeep carrying large milk cans full of water. Jalopies and trucks, every car in town followed carrying water in whatever could hold it. Up they sped, but being careful not to run down the parade of little animals. This was not the first time that the village had put out a forest fire. On the cars careened. Down went the mountain creatures.

When the fire was under control, when the last of the cars had come down the mountain, and the mountain creatures had started home, back up the trail, Flickertail still lingered on at the foot of the mountain. He had met Skunk and a friend, the roadside skunk, and they chattered, going over the great event. After picking up a few scattered crumbs left around the snack bar, where coffee and sandwiches were offered the fire brigade, the three watched from beneath bushes as the cars turned slowly home.

"We saw you coming along, waving your tail like a torch, Mr. Flick." Skunk said. "We admire you. We feel that you saved the day."

"Oh, I would not say that," Flickertail tossed off the compliment. "I only used my tail in an emergency." He had not realized before that his golden tail had been a bright banner for the mountain creatures to follow through the smoke.

They watched Early Ford, with a good-by toot, start on his homeward way. "You won't come up with me for a call, Skunk, you and your friend?" he asked. "I don't think the fire did much damage." Then he remembered. He had asked Coon to take shelter in the Cranny. It was hardly large enough for all of them.

"Thank you, Mr. Flick," Skunk replied. "Thank you ever so much, but we find it a longer walk than we can undertake. Your feet must be hardened to the trail by now, but we find it softer and pleasanter down here at the snack bar, which serves big suppers for us. It was pleasant, though, to see you, Mr. Flick."

Flickertail looked up along the way he had come. If he was a hero, as he did not admit, certainly Early Ford had been one. It had meant dangerous and brave going to get

Early Ford up the long trail to the edge of the fire, to wait in the smoke while the potato sacks were wetted and put to work.

All his friends, Flickertail felt, were safe. The Beavers had their waterway and so did the frogs. The others would have their burrows. The Cranny was a comfortable and well-stocked home for Coon, who had never had a real home of his own, camping in hollow trees or in other creatures' burrows. The shelves in the Cranny that Flickertail had used for his food would serve Coon nicely. There he could keep ears of dried corn and shell beans. He knew the Cranny would serve Coon's problem of how to spend the winter. He had, so to speak, sublet it. Flickertail realized that, for the second time that season, he was without a real home. This was not new for Flickertail. All his life he had been moving, from mountain to mountain, from hill to valley, from city to village.

The two skunks now lurked at the entrance to the snack bar. Of course Flickertail could stay with them, but their habits were different from his. Hearing Early Ford's rattle had brought old times to his mind. But at the Old Place he had been a stranger, unwanted, even unseen most of the time. He was now, so to speak, at a crossroads.

Flickertail looked about him. Above towered the mountain, smoking, but still a place of happiness and content. Beyond lay the long and dusty road that led to town. The day was now beginning to cool into sunset and evening. His feet were less hot now, and he could pick up a juicy meal of twigs along the road. He could sleep soundly beside First Brook that, down here, flowed into Second Brook. Bushes would shelter him through the night.

Flickertail made a decision. He started toward town.

10 · At Home

THE VILLAGE general store was an exciting place. Towns-people brought in things to sell—maple syrup, eggs, fresh butter, cream. They brought news also of the town's doings. Others, buying sugar for canning, hamburgers, frankfurters and bacon, carried out and spread the news. This bright morning early in September the store was full, business going on briskly and interesting conversation also.

Ann and Timothy were there.

Timothy, a town boy, was always around, haying, mowing lawns, picking berries, being generally useful. Ann had been at the Cape with the family, but she had not liked it as much as the Old Place. Now, since she was going to Boston to boarding school shortly, she had come home on the bus. She was boarding with Timothy's mother and helping to open the Old Place until the rest of the family returned. She and Timothy, having been friends for a long time, had ever so much to talk about. They were at the back of the store when conversation that surprised them interrupted.

"I hear the little varmint's back in town." That was old Mr. Mountain who had brought in a basket of Mrs. Mountain's ginger cookies to barter for the spice she needed for her ketchup. "He's been seen hanging around the Old Place."

Ann and Timothy moved near the center of the talk, their ears open.

"Yes. He came back a while ago," the storekeeper said. "Some saw him coming down the mountain, the day of the fire, lickety-split, waving his tail, a crowd of little animals who never come down the trail, foxes, quill pigs, deer, racoons following. I don't belittle our fire brigade, but I would say he did his share in warning of the fire."

"Who?" Ann asked.

"The squirrel with the yellow tail," Timothy told her. "I've heard of him. He was seen hereabouts in the early summer, but I didn't pay much heed. I've been busy, Ann. I've saved money to go over to the Academy this term. I've been earning my tuition. Anyway, that freak animal disappeared early this summer. I'm too old for fairy tales, and most people said he was just that."

Other customers went on with the report. Some had seen him and some had not. Those who had, kept quiet about it for fear they would be laughed at. The pastor thought he had seen him. Some boys on the Common remembered they had seen him and gotten a rifle, but then had met up with a skunk, which put them off his trail. "Anyway, he's been seen lately, still wearing that tail," the storekeeper said.

Just then Ann saw something exciting, a pile of red and white striped paper bags, a new item in the store's delightful goods. "Peanuts," she shouted. "Timothy, the darling Nuttings! Alone all summer. Let's take them a bag." The news of the fire on the mountain passed out of her thoughts as she bought a bag of the peanuts.

"Let's. I'll walk over with you," he said.

She and Timothy left the store and started along the road that led beside fields and orchards up to the rise of ground that held her beloved Old Place.

They sat, the Nutting family of squirrels, in a circle on the door-stone of the Old Place. They were plump and lively, talking earnestly in a close group. Flickertail sat next to Mr. Nutting, who rested a friendly paw on Flickertail's head. He now seemed genial. "Flick, my boy," Mr. Nutting said, seeming to have lost his aversion to the stranger, "now you're here, don't think of going farther. Stay with us. Be one of us."

"Yes, do." Mrs. Nutting agreed happily with Mr. Nutting. "We have a spare room here in the Porter apple tree. It is ready for you, spread with fresh moss and leaves. The bed is made up, and we would be proud to have you."

"School opens next week," Miss Bushy Nutting said. "You can teach a class of beginning geography. You have traveled far and have the experience that I lack. You will broaden their minds."

Willie spoke now. "Long winter evenings, Flick, you can join me in the attic. The heat rises, and it is one of the warmest rooms in the house. There are shelves and shelves of books that I have not had time to touch—travel, the poets, *Youth's Companion*, good gnawing all of them."

Flickertail considered. His summer on the mountain had been wonderful, but he had never in his past life had such a family, never a welcome such as this. After the fire he had said good-by to the two skunks. He walked and leaped his way from the foot of Temple Mountain, sleeping beside the road, going back along the way he had come. He had had in mind calling on Early Ford in the barn of the Old Place and congratulating him on his share in putting out the fire. He had had no intention of staying in town. He felt he would not be welcomed.

He had been greatly surprised as he came to the outskirts of town that no one chased him. Indeed he seemed to be expected and generally welcomed. No longer had he any need of skulking or climbing trees. Those whom he met seemed to admire him. They stopped to look with what seemed to be approval at his tail. He came bravely toward the Old Place in the middle of the road, waving his tail.

He had chattered in the barn to Early Ford whose paint, being scorched, must be giving him a little pain. Flickertail considered living again in the barn, but he had gone outside and found himself made welcome by the Nuttings. For news of the fire had spread, and Flickertail was a hero.

The talk there was suddenly broken by the arrival of Grandpa Nutting, who had been forgotten in the turn the talk had taken. Grandpa was limping with more speed than seemed possible at his age. His heart was beating like a hammer. He landed with a leap in the center of the family

circle. He took something from his cheek that made him look as if he had mumps on one side only. He took it out and gave the treasure to Flickertail. "A peanut, Flick!" he chattered. "The whole back lawn is strewn with peanuts. I brought you one before I ate any myself."

There was a pause. Then, led by Willie, the Nuttings left as one squirrel. Flickertail remained, holding his peanut in his paws.

Flickertail opened the shell and ate the nuts slowly, one at a time. They tasted of all the rich meals he had missed during his travels. Also, they had another flavor, that of the kindness that he had missed for so long a time. He sniffed the flavor left in the shell, thinking.

Here he was offered a home. He could be useful here. That the Nuttings had told him. And they really seemed to want him. He had been happy on the mountain, but any time he wanted to he could pay the mountain a visit. His friends there were safe and well housed; the fire had not damaged their trees or burrows too much. A winter of sleep, another spring, and the mountain would be green and rich in food for them again. Here, Flickertail thought, he was needed.

In addition to the duties the Nuttings had suggested, he would see what he could do about Grandpa Nutting's tail. Regular combing and brushing with pine cones might improve it, make the hairs come in again. He would not neglect his friend of old, Early Ford, who had suffered in putting out the forest fire. He would visit him in the barn and tell him of pleasant days on the mountain. All in all, it seemed to Flickertail like the happiest of endings. And there were more peanuts out back.

With a feeling that his empty peanut shell was a souvenir, Flickertail hid it in Mrs. Nutting's spare room. Then he ran, leaped, and sprinted around the corner of the Old Place. Flickertail Nutting joined his family.